Adventures with Peppa

Published by arrangement with Entertainment One and Ladybird Books, A Penguin
Company. This book is based on the TV series *Peppa Pig*.
Peppa Pig is created by Neville Astley and Mark Baker.
Peppa Pig © Astley Baker Davies Ltd/Entertainment One UK Ltd 2003.

Peppa Pig™: Little Creatures (978-0-545-92624-9)
© Astley Baker Davies Ltd/Entertainment One UK Ltd 2003.

Peppa Pig™: Nature Trail (978-0-545-92623-2)
© Astley Baker Davies Ltd/Entertainment One UK Ltd 2003.

Peppa Pig™: Class Trip (978-0-545-52402-5)
© Astley Baker Davies Ltd/Entertainment One UK Ltd 2003.

Peppa Pig™: Peppa Goes Swimming (978-0-545-83491-9)
© Astley Baker Davies Ltd/Entertainment One UK Ltd 2003.

ISBN 978-0-545-92625-6

10 9 8 7 6 5   16 17 18 19 20

Printed in China   38
First printing 2015

Contents

Meet the Characters:

Peppa

George

Grandpa Pig

Granny Pig

Mummy Pig

Daddy Pig

Little Creatures

Little Creatures

Adapted version written by
Lorraine Horsley

This is Peppa.

This is George.
George is her little brother.

This is Grandpa Pig and this is
Granny Pig.

Peppa, George, and Grandpa Pig are in the garden.

Grandpa Pig gives Peppa a head of lettuce.

"What is that?" asks Peppa.

"It is a snail," says Grandpa Pig.

George likes the snail.

"Where is the snail now, Grandpa?"
asks Peppa.

"It is in its shell," says Grandpa Pig.
"The shell is the snail's little house."

George wants to be a snail in a little house.

"I want to be a snail in a little house, too!" says Peppa. "Grandpa, we will eat your lettuce!"

Now Peppa and George's friends are in the garden, too.

Buzz! Buzz! Buzz!

"What is that?" they ask.

"Bumblebees," says Grandpa Pig.

"Where are they going?" asks Peppa.

"They are going to make some honey," says Grandpa Pig.

"I like honey!" says Peppa.

The friends want to be bees.

"*Buzz! Buzz! Buzz!*" they say.

Granny Pig comes to the garden.
Granny Pig gives Peppa and her
friends some honey and toast
to eat.

"I like bees," says Peppa.

"We like bees, too," say Peppa's friends. "We like to eat the honey they make!"

How much do you remember about *Peppa Pig*™: *Little Creatures?* Answer these questions and find out!

- What does Grandpa Pig give Peppa?

- Who likes the snail?

- Where are the bees going?

- What does Granny Pig give Peppa and her friends to eat?

Look at the pictures from the story and say the order they should go in.

Answer: C, A, D, B

Nature Trail

Adapted version written by
Lorraine Horsley

Peppa Pig and her family are going on a picnic in the woods.

Daddy Pig has the map.

In the woods, Peppa sees something on the ground.

"Look down there!" says Peppa. "I see footprints on the ground!"

Peppa and her family follow the footprints.

"A bird made these footprints," says Mummy Pig.

"Look up there in the tree!" says Peppa. "I see some birds!"

There is a mommy bird and three little birds up in the tree.

Then Peppa sees more little
footprints on the ground.

"Look down there!" says
Peppa. "I see some ants!"

Peppa and her family are hungry. They need to eat but the picnic basket is in the car.

Daddy Pig looks at the map. "I don't know the way back to the car," he says.

Then it rains.

The rain takes all the footprints away.

"I know!" says Peppa. "I see some ducks over there. Ducks love the rain AND they love picnics. We can follow these ducks back to the food in our car!"

"I love picnics in the woods!" says Peppa.

The birds, the ants, and the ducks love the picnic, too!

How much do you remember about *Peppa Pig™: Nature Trail*? Answer these questions and find out!

- Where do Peppa and her family go for a picnic?

- What does Peppa see in the woods?

- Why do the family's footprints go away?

- Who shows Peppa and her family the way back to the car?

Look at the pictures and match them to the words from the story.

birds

Mummy Pig

ants

George

Peppa

Daddy Pig

ducks

Class Trip

Adapted version written by
Ellen Philpott

Peppa and her friends are going
on a school trip.

Woof!

"Is everyone here?" asks Madame Gazelle.

"Yes," they say.

Everyone loves school trips.

"Where are we going for our trip?"
asks Peppa.

"We are going to the mountains,"
says Madame Gazelle.

"Hooray!" everyone cheers.

The bus is going to the top of a big mountain. It is very high up.

"Come on, bus!" says Peppa.

Up, up, up they go.

The bus gets to the top and everyone gets out.

"Come and look at the big mountains," says Madame Gazelle.

Peppa looks at the mountains. She is very high up.

"Wow," she says.

Everyone hears, "Wow, wow, wow."

"What was that?" asks Peppa.

"That was an echo", says Madame Gazelle. "It is what you hear when you call out, up in the mountains."

"Come on, everyone," says Peppa.
"We can all make an echo."

The children call out, "Wow."
Then they hear, "Wow, wow, wow."

"Come on, children," says
Madame Gazelle. "It is time for
our picnic."

"Hooray!" everyone cheers.

"Where are the ducks?" asks Peppa.
"They love it when we have picnics,
too."

Peppa and her friends look out for the ducks.

Quack! Quack! Quack! Here come the
ducks!
"Hello! Would you like some bread?"
Peppa asks them.

The ducks are very lucky today. The kids brought plenty of extra bread to feed them!

"Come here, ducks," says Madame Gazelle.

"Yes, join our picnic, ducks," says Peppa.

The ducks have a big picnic, too.

It is time to go back to school. The children get on the bus. Then they sing a song as they go back down the mountain.

Everyone loves school trips!

Everyone loves school bus trips!

How much do you remember about *Peppa Pig™: Class Trip?*
Answer these questions and find out!

- Where do Peppa and her friends go?

- What do the children do on the bus?

- What does everyone hear when Peppa says, "Wow"?

- What do the children feed the ducks?

Look at the pictures and match them
to the words from the story.

mountain

bus

picnic

ducks

Madame Gazelle

Peppa Goes Swimming

Peppa Goes Swimming

Adapted version written by
Scholastic

It is a warm summer day.

Peppa and her family are at the
swimming pool.

"Peppa, George, let Daddy put on your swimming armbands," says Mummy Pig.

Today is George's first time at the pool. He's scared of getting in the water.

"Why don't you put just one foot in?" asks Daddy Pig.

"Maybe George should try both feet at the same time," says Mummy Pig.

"Grunt! Hee! Hee! Snort!" shouts
George happily.

"Ho! Ho! Well done, George!"
snorts Daddy Pig.

Rebecca Rabbit, her brother, Richard, and their mother arrive at the pool, too.

"Richard, hold on to this float. You can practice kicking your legs," says Mrs. Rabbit.

"George, would you like to try kicking your legs, too?" asks Mummy Pig.

"Hee! Hee! Snort!" giggles George.

"Big children are good at swimming," says Peppa. "When George and Richard are older, they will be able to swim like us. Won't they, Rebecca?"

"Yes!" says Rebecca. She watches the
boys kick and splash.

Peppa and Rebecca race each other up and down the pool with their swimming armbands on.

They have lots of fun swimming and splashing in the water!

Oops! Richard dropped his toy watering can into the pool.

"Mummy! Wah!" cries Richard.

"Sorry, Richard, I can't reach it. It's too far down," says Mrs. Rabbit.

Luckily, Daddy Pig is an excellent swimmer. He takes off his glasses and dives down to get Richard's watering can.

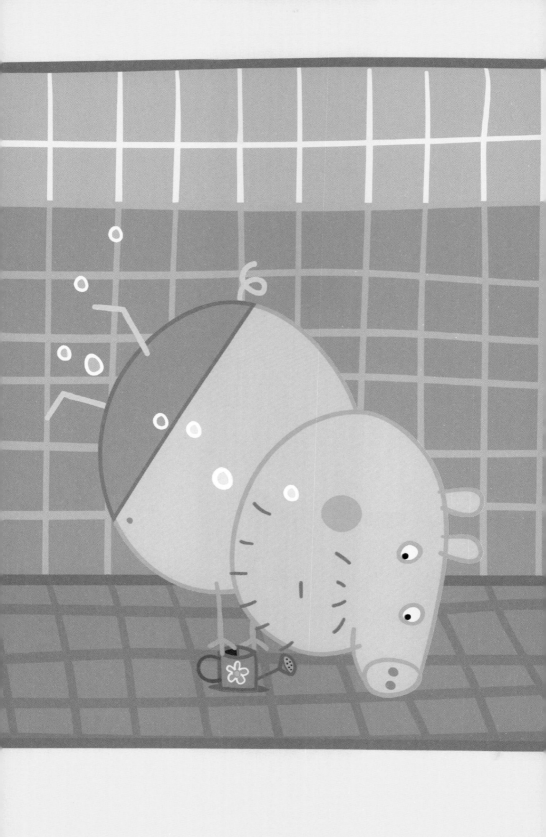

"Ho! Ho! There you go!" Daddy Pig snorts.

"Squeak, squeak!" says Richard.

"Well done, Daddy Pig!" says Mummy Pig.

"Thank you, Daddy Pig," says Mrs. Rabbit.

Oh, dear! Richard is so happy to have his watering can back that he splashes Daddy Pig with water!

"Hee! Hee! Hee!" George laughs.

What a silly little piggy and rabbit!

Everyone had fun swimming at the pool!

How much do you remember about *Peppa Pig™: Peppa Goes Swimming*? Answer these questions and find out!

- What do Peppa and George wear when they go swimming?

- How do George and Richard practice kicking their legs?

- What does Richard drop to the bottom of the pool?

- Who helps Richard get back what he dropped?